This book belongs to
my friend:

_____

A NOTE TO PARENTS

Preschool children often experiment with make-believe play. It helps them explore the world as well as themselves. In *A Rainy Day to Remember*, Little Bill relies on his imagination to chase away the rainy day blues. In doing so, he learns to draw on his inner resources to make the best of a disappointing situation.

As you explore the story with your child, engage his imagination by asking, "When you play make-believe, what do you pretend to be or to do?" Encourage your child to put himself in Little Bill's shoes. "If you were Little Bill, what would you do to make a rainy day fun?"

Rainy days or times of boredom happen to all children. Try to be prepared for such times. Collect props—old clothes, sheets, safe household items—and store them in a box ready for play. Ideas and instructions for kid-friendly recipes, easy crafts, and games can be kept on note cards for easy access. Use your imagination to come up with lots of other rainy day ideas!

Learning Fundamental: **imagination**

For more parent and kid-friendly activities, go to www.nickjr.com.

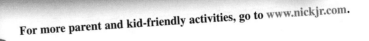

"I'm going to the park with Andrew today," he continued. "We're going to sail boats on the pond and play dinosaurs and build a super-high sand fort. It can't rain today!"

Little Bill's mother put an arm around his shoulder. "I'm sorry, baby," she said, "you and Andrew will have to play inside today."

"But there's nothing to do here," Little Bill sighed.

"I'm sure you'll think of something to do. You'll just have to use your imagination," his mother said. "How about we start with breakfast? Alice the Great is making your favorite pancake people."

Little Bill joined his sister, April, and his brother, Bobby, at the kitchen table. His great-grandmother, Alice the Great, put a plate of pancakes in front of him.

Little Bill's mother came into the room. "Good morning, baby," she said. "Did you sleep well?"
"Mama, it's raining!" said Little Bill.

A Rainy Day to Remember

Published by Scholastic Inc., 90 Old Sherman Turnpike, Danbury, CT 06816

ISBN 0-7172-6620-6

Printed in the U.S.A.

First Scholastic Printing, September 2002

A Rainy Day to Remember

by
Kitty Fross

illustrated by
Jennifer Oxley

SCHOLASTIC INC.

New York   Toronto   London   Auckland   Sydney
Mexico City   New Delhi   Hong Kong   Buenos Aires

Plink! Splink-a-dink!

Little Bill opened his eyes. "What's that sound?" he wondered. He hopped out of bed and pulled back the curtains. Raindrops were bouncing off the window, and the sky was a dull, dark gray.

"Oh, no!" said Little Bill. "It can't be raining! Not today!"

"Here you go, honey. I made their heads extra big, just the way you like them," she said.

Little Bill poured syrup on his pancakes
and began pushing them around his plate with
his fork. Bobby looked over and pointed at one
with an enormous head.

"Hey, Little Bill. That pancake looks like an alien!" Bobby said.

"Wow!" said Little Bill. "You're right!"

In the blink of an eye, Little Bill's plate
turned into a spaceship, and the pancake people
became real, live aliens!

Little Bill imagined himself flying the spaceship
through outer space.

"We're coming in for a landing!" called Captain Little Bill. "Oh, no! Look out for that lake!"
Sploosh! Little Bill's spaceship skidded through a giant lake of syrup and came to a sticky stop.

Little Bill giggled and took a bite of pancake. "Mmm, these aliens are delicious!" he told Alice the Great.

After breakfast, Little Bill went to his room
to wait for Andrew. "I still wish we could play
dinosaurs today," he thought to himself.
Suddenly he had an idea. "Hey, I can make
a picture of a dinosaur!" he exclaimed.

"*Roarrrrrr! Roarrrrrr!*" growled Little Bill as he drew.
"I'm a giant Rainosaurus! My voice is like thunder!"

April walked past Little Bill's room.
"That's a great drawing, Little Bill," she said.
"You should show it to Mama!"

"Good idea!" said Little Bill. He ran downstairs, carefully holding his drawing.

Little Bill found his mother in the laundry room, putting clothes in the dryer. A pile of sheets sat on the washer. He had another idea. "Mama, can I make a fort with these sheets?" he asked.

"Yes you may, Little Bill," his mother answered. Little Bill carried the sheets and his drawing into the living room. He leaned the Rainosaurus against the sofa and draped the sheets over some chairs.

Just then the doorbell rang. Andrew and
his mother stood on the steps.
  "Why, come in Andrew!" said Alice the Great.
"Take off those wet things."

Andrew took off his boots and
jacket. "Where's Little Bill?" he asked.
Little Bill burrowed inside his sheet fort.
"Hey, Andrew," he called, "bet you can't find me!"

Andrew ran over and peeked under the flap. "Hi, Little Bill," he said. "Too bad it's too wet to go to the park."

Little Bill nodded. "But I built a really neat fort in here, and it's nice and dry inside," he said. "Yeah," said Andrew, "it's *really* neat!"

Andrew threw a sheet over his
head and waved his arms. "Look, Little Bill! I'm a
ghost. *Whoooooo!*" he said in a spooky voice.

Little Bill giggled. He wrapped a sheet around himself like a robe. "Yeah, and I'm the king!" he said. "We have to save the kingdom from the terrible Rainosaurus!"

Andrew pulled his sheet off his head. "I can jump in and scare the Rainosaurus away!" he said.

"Me, too!" said Little Bill.
"Let's save the kingdom!" they shouted.

A while later, Little Bill's mother
peeked into the room. "The rain stopped," she
told the boys. "Who wants to go to the park?"
Little Bill and Andrew looked at each other.
"Mama, can we stay inside?" Little Bill asked.
"We still have lots of stuff to do here."

His mother smiled. "Of course, Little Bill. You can stay inside as long as you like."

So Little Bill and Andrew played and played until they'd saved the whole kingdom.

It was a rainy day they'd never forget.